Taking Turns

By Dawn McMillan

Illustrated by Julia Marshall

Jake and Liam went to the park.

"We can play on the swing," said Liam.

"I'm going first!"

Liam ran to the swing.

"Here I go!" shouted Liam.
"Look at me!
I am going up."

The swing went up and up.

Then it went back down again.

Up
and
down.

Up
and
down.

Jake said, "Can I play
on the swing too?"

"No!" said Liam.
"This is my swing today."
"I like this swing."

"I'm not going to play with you!"
said Jake.
He went away.

Liam looked at Jake.

"Come here, Jake," he said.

"You can play on the swing."

Liam jumped off the swing.

"Here you are, Jake," he said.

"You can go on the swing now."

"Good!" said Jake.

"I will swing up like you.

Can you help me, please, Liam?"

The swing went up and up.

"Look at me!" shouted Jake.

The swing went down and down.

"I will stop it for you," said Liam.

"You can go on the swing now,"
said Jake.

"This is a good way to play!"
said Liam.